ROBROY
LIBRARY

Nº 13

1ᵈ

THE WOLF OF RANNOCH.

"'To whom have I the honour?' asked Rob Roy, composedly.
'You are a prisoner of the Wolf of Rannoch,' replied the masked
man."

THE WOLF OF RANNOCH.

By ANGUS MACLEAN.

CHAPTER I.

THE MYSTERIOUS HORSEMAN.

HELP! Help! Help!

A woman's despairing cry rang out amongst the hills of Perthshire, startling the moorfowl from their heathery lair.

As the wailing echoes reverberated through the glens, two Highlanders, who had been resting on the heath, sprang to their feet.

They stood and listened with bated breath, but no sound save the rushing waters in the glen reached their ears.

"I could have sworn," said the taller of the two, a majestic man armed with claymore, dirk and targe. "I could have sworn I heard a woman's cry for help."

"That's what I thought, Rob," replied the other; "but it might have been the scream of the curlew."

"No, no, Alastair," replied the other, softly and quickly, still straining his ears. "No, no; it was a woman's voice, and it came from the direction of Ben More. Come, let us climb the hill and see."

Rob Roy, for it was he, sprang up the hill side, followed by Alastair, his brother.

"What would a woman want in these wilds," ejaculated Alastair as he gained Rob Roy's side.

"That's exactly what I want to know," said Rob Roy, as he continued to climb rapidly.

"Look," he exclaimed, as he gained the top, and pointed towards the slopes of the distant mountain of Ben More.

Both instantly unslung their telescopes. Round the bend of the hill a horseman was galloping at a furious rate.

"By heaven," exclaimed Rob Roy, as he steadied his glass, "he has a woman thrown across his knees."

"A woman," repeated Alastair, "with golden flowing tresses."

"And the scoundrel has his hand over her mouth," growled Roy Roy. "Curse him; he is beyond rifle shot."

"Or he would go down in a trice," interpolated Alastair.

"That accounts for our not hearing another cry," said Rob Roy, as the horseman disappeared from view. "Did you note his dress, Alastair?"

"I did, brother Rob," replied Alastair. "He is not a Highlander. He wore the hunting dress of the Saxon."

"And he rides a Saxon horse—a fine one, too," interjected Roy Roy.

"That means foul play then," said Alastair, "for it shows premeditation."

"How so?" asked Rob Roy.

"Because for fifty miles around there are no horses like that—only mettlesome mountain ponies. He has brought the horse from the lowlands, and that shows the Saxon is playing a part in some deep laid scheme."

"Exactly what I think," replied Rob Roy, knitting his brows; "but why is the man in this vicinity?"

"He rides due north," said Alastair. "And right through the lands of the MacGregor," interjected Rob Roy. "There is some mystery here. Alastair, we must fathom this. Go as quickly as you can to the Clachan, and bring six men with you. Follow my trail. Meanwhile, I shall follow in the track of that mysterious horseman. The woman must be saved at all costs."

In a moment Rob Roy bounded down the hillside.

"Tell Mary I shall be back in a couple of days," he shouted over his shoulder, as he descended rapidly.

Little did he dream that many days were to pass before he saw his darling wife again.

CHAPTER II.

THE MYSTERY DEEPENS.

Making for the spot where he last saw the mysterious horseman, Rob Roy soon struck the trail, and followed it like a sleuth-hound.

To an experienced mountaineer and woodsman like Rob Roy, the trail presented no difficulty.

Unlike the mountain ponies of the Highlands, the horse on which the kidnapper rode was shod, and left distinct marks on the soft ground.

Rob Roy pressed forward at a swinging pace, and did not stop until he had covered many miles.

"This is a longer journey than I bargained for," exclaimed Rob Roy, as he pulled off his plumed bonnet, and wiped his heated brow. "But now that I have commenced, I shall see it through to the end."

Drawing his wallet from his back, he helped himself to a piece of dried deer's flesh, and washing it down with a draught of clear cold water from the brook close at hand, he recommenced his journey.

Coming to a piece of stony ground, interspersed here and there with a few struggling trees, he found no traces of the mysterious horseman. But Rob Roy was not the man to be discomfited.

Marking the place where he stood, he searched the ground systematically in a circle, and was rewarded for his diligence by rediscovering the trail.

"It is quite simple," laughed Rob Roy. "The man, whoever he is, has made no attempt to prevent pursuit. He is evidently in a hurry."

Rob Roy drew his dirk, and cut a very small piece of his red tartan plaid, and fixed in on the lower branches of a tree near by. Then quickly placing five stones one behind the other on the ground directly below the tree, he set off once more.

"That will give the clue to Alastair when he follows," muttered Rob Roy. "The track now leads towards Rannoch."

The country through which Rob Roy now passed was wild in the extreme, but he quickly followed the horse's tracks along the well-defined valley, bordered by rocky eminences scattered over the country in tumultous confusion.

Still Rob Roy pushed forward, and the waning light of day still saw him striding along at a swinging pace. Suddenly he stopped as he emerged from a narrow gully between the rocks. His quick eye had detected a movement amongst the bushes in front.

Instantly a figure sprang from behind the bushes and covered Rob Roy's body with a long barrelled Spanish rifle.

"Stand! You are my prisoner!" exclaimed the figure in a loud voice.

The man was not a Highlander. His long black hair hung in matted locks on his shoulders; his hunting shirt, originally saffron coloured, was bleached by exposure to wind and rain to all hues of the rainbow, and his wide trousers hung in tatters. He was weather-beaten and grimy, but the rifle he held in his corded brown hand, and the pistols and the knife in his belt, together with the cruel rowel spurs that helped in a manner to support his ragged nether garments were bright, and clean, and serviceable.

"Stand! You are my prisoner!" he thundered.

"A Saxon," muttered Rob Roy, as he looked down the barrel of the gun not five yards from him.

"Why am I your prisoner," demanded Rob Roy, "and what want you in the Highlands?"

"That is my business," replied the other, curtly. "Throw your sword and pistols on the ground or in a moment you will die."

Rob Roy was non-plussed. What a man, dressed like his enemy, was doing in the wilds of Rannoch he could not imagine. At the same time Rob Roy knew that the man had him at an advantage.

"Quick!" ordered the man. "Throw down your sword."

Rob Roy had no intention of doing so, but he drew his claymore, and, instead of throwing it on the ground, he hurled it with terrific force at the man, who was completely taken aback by the sudden movement.

He staggered under the blow, and unconsciously pulled the trigger. Before the echoes of the shot had died away, Rob Roy had sprung at him and pinned him to the ground.

"Now," said Rob Roy, as he coolly squatted on the man's body, "it is my turn. You are my prisoner. If you answer a few questions I put to you I shall spare your life. If not, this will be your fate." And Rob Roy touched the man's throat with the cold steel of his dirk.

"Let me up," groaned the man, "you are choking me with your weight. Let me up, and I will answer."

"Wait one minute, then," replied Rob Roy, who saw that the man was really injured. Quickly Rob Roy drew the pistols from the man's belt, and running his fingers over his hunting-shirt pulled out a formidable knife.

Throwing them on the ground, Rob Roy rose. "Sit up," he said, "but on the pain of death do not attempt to rise."

"I am not likely to rise in a hurry," laughed the man, sardonically, pointing at the same time to a wound on his head from which the blood was flowing.

Rob Roy had a tender heart. Drawing his sharp dirk he cut the matted locks of the man round the wound. With nimble fingers he dressed the injury.

"It is only flesh deep," he said. "Lucky for you that the hilt of the claymore struck you. Had it been the blade your case would have been hopeless. Now, answer my questions, and as you wish to live, answer truly."

"I will," replied the man, as he gazed up at Rob Roy. Despite his weather-beaten appearance, he was not a bad looking fellow.

"Who are you and what is your name?" demanded Rob Roy.

"I am a Dane, and my name is Jorgenson."

"A Dane!" exclaimed Rob Roy, in surprise. "You speak English well."

"I have been with the English all my life. I was a sailor," replied Jorgensen.

"And what on earth are you doing here?" asked Rob Roy.

"That is more than I can tell you?" replied Jorgensen, with a laugh.

"Don't trifle with me," said Rob Roy, sternly. "What are you doing here?"

"And I tell you," replied the man, somewhat tartly, "it is more than I can tell you."

"You mean," said Rob Roy, threateningly, "that you refuse to tell me."

"No, I do not refuse," answered Jorgensen, "I will tell you what I know."

"Then, how came you here?" demanded Rob Roy.

"All I know about the affair is this," said Jorgensen. "I told you I was a sailor; I was more. I was wrecked in the West Indies, and was picked up by a band of men under a Welshman, named Morgan. They were pirates. I joined their band, and we lived on plunder on the Spanish galleons."

"One moment," interrupted Rob Roy. "Have you any comrades near?"

"Not within three miles that I know of," replied Jorgensen.

"Walk over to these rocks," said Rob Roy, pointing to the sides of the gully. "Sit with your back to the rocks. We shall be out of sight, and I shall be better able to guard against surprise. Proceed."

"We lived on the Spanish galleons," continued Jorgensen. "After a few years, when we had collected a lot of money, half a dozen of us determined to give up the life and return to England. Morgan was willing to allow us to go after we had given an oath not to divulge any secrets, and accordingly we rigged up a barque. But the very night before we were going to start, Morgan's lieutenant, named Twaite, deserted with the ship, taking with him some twenty of the worst of the pirates. What became of them we never knew. They took away with them the savings of ten years."

"Then what happened?" asked Rob Roy.

"We still had the idea of giving up the life—so had Morgan—and in three years time the same half-dozen saved what we could, and this time there was no mistake. We slept on board the barque—one captured from the Spaniards—and set sail. We encountered rough weather, were driven off our course, and were shipwrecked on the rocks of the coast which afterwards turned out to be the island of Tiree."

"I know it," interpolated Rob Roy, "I have seen it from the mountains of Mull."

"Only three of us were saved, and we were taken to a cave. Our rescuers were evidently smugglers, and judge my surprise when one of the men in the cave turned out to be one-eyed Peter. He was Twaite's right-hand man. There and then we had to take the oath, swearing loyalty to the band of wreckers, but anyway, in three days' time I was blindfolded, taken a long journey, and arrived here where you find me."

"A nice fairy tale," said Rob Roy, drily, "and for what purpose?"

"Five hundred yards from here you will find a hut concealed in the face of the glen. It was there when I came. Those who brought me wore masks, so that I did not know them, and my orders were that I should take up my post here to prevent any one, no matter whom, from entering the glen."

"Why?" asked Rob Roy.

"That I do not know," was Jorgensen's reply, "but this I do know that my orders are also that I do not move away under any pretence more than half a mile from my post. If I do the penalty is death."

"And you ask me to believe this story!" exclaimed Rob Roy.

"I do," replied Jorgenson, with much seriousness. "I do indeed. Listen. I want to get back to the sea, and one night I determined to escape. I had not gone three quarters of a mile west when I was challenged. I pretended I had been following a suspicious person, but the lie was not believed, and I was told by a masked man that escape was useless. If I wished to live I had to stick to my post in the meantime."

"But supposing," said Rob Roy, "that you wished to communicate with headquarters or the head of the band, what do you do?"

Jorgenson pointed to a pile of dried brushwood. "There!" he exclaimed. "Set fire to that. But every day a masked patrol visits me. I never know when. Sometimes it is in the early part of the day, sometimes at night."

"From what direction do they come?" asked Rob Roy.

"Generally from the north; but there is no telling. All I know is that if I

allow any one to pass up the glen it means death to me."

"But there is nothing beyond the glen. At least there was not several years ago. Only a bleak, mountainous country," said Rob Roy.

"That I do not know; I have never been there," replied Jorgenson.

"But what is the meaning of it all?" asked Rob Roy. "You said you were taken from Tiree."

"I was. I am as much mystified as you."

"But cannot you guess at anything?"

"Nothing, unless Twaite is in England, and up to his devilish tricks. He is equal to any thing."

"But," objected Rob Roy, "I cannot see what he could have to do with anything here. Beyond there is but the wild uninhabited district of Rannoch."

"Is it near the sea?" asked Jorgensen, eagerly.

"It is not near the sea," replied Rob Roy, "but it is no great distance from it. It is an easy journey to Loch Leven, and onward through Loch Linnhe to the sea."

Jorgensen shook his head. "It is a mystery to me," he said, "I wish I could escape."

"You can escape if you care," said Rob Roy.

"How?" exclaimed Jorgensen, eagerly.

"By simply keeping direct to the south."

Jorgensen again shook his head.

"No," he said, "I was told that I should walk right into the principal piquet of the band if I did so."

"That is all wrong!" exclaimed Rob Roy. "Now, I shall make an offer. You say you wish to escape from your unknown masters. In any case the penalty is death, for I am determined to probe this mystery to the bottom. I am going forward through the glen, and you say you will be killed for allowing me; very well, then. You set out at once, keep direct south, and you will meet my brother, Alastair, and his men following my track. Tell him to make all haste."

"There is one thing I had forgotten to tell you," said Jorgensen.

"And what is that?" asked Rob Roy.

"A horseman passed here early this morning."

Rob Roy whistled. "I must be getting in my dotage," he said. "I had forgotten for the moment about him. Where did he pass ? "

" Along the gully, and onwards through the glen."

" But I thought you were to allow no one to pass ? "

" The masked patrol gave me warning three days ago that a horseman, perhaps accompanied by a woman, might pass at any time. I was to let him go without question."

" Who was he ? " asked Rob Roy.

" I do not know. He was masked, and rode at a gallop. A girl was in his arms across the saddle bow."

" What do you think of it ? "

" A case of kidnapping."

" But where to ? "

Jorgensen shook his head. " The masked patrol said nothing this morning."

" Well, look here," said Rob Roy, " my name is Rob Roy."

" I have heard of you," interrupted Jorgensen, " and when I was leaving Tiree I overheard one-eyed Peter say that the only difficulty was if the MacGregors came to hear of the place. What place I do not know."

" I am giving you a chance," continued Rob Roy. " You look honest enough, and I am trusting you. Start, at once, southwards ; tell my brother, Alastair, to hurry forward. Give him all information, and tell him to be careful. I am going forward. Daybreak may bring forth something."

" MacGregor," said Jorgensen, gravely, " I have heard of your brave heart, but if you go forward you go to your death."

" He is an old friend of mine," laughed Rob Roy. " I have been looking him in the face daily for the past few years, so I am not afraid to meet him now. Go forward. When we meet again I shall see that you once more get on board ship, when you can once more begin a respectable life. Go at once."

Jorgensen rose and held out his hand. Rob Roy shook it warmly. " That settles it," he said.

Rob Roy watched Jorgensen out of sight. But he was not the only one who was watching. The keen eyes of the leader of the masked patrol were gleaming through his mask, as he lay concealed among the brushwood that flanked the glen.

CHAPTER III.

CAPTURED.

" So there is treachery in the band," muttered the leader of the masked patrol. " It is what I expected. The chief should have shot these men as I recommended when they were cast ashore. We are never safe, and I suspected that Jorgensen from the beginning, when one-eyed Peter told me the fool always wanted to give up his life of freedom. We shall see what we shall see, and this MacGregor chieftain must be captured.

" Ha ! " continued the patrol leader, " I have a plan. The English Government offers a reward of £1,000 for his capture, and why should not I get it as well as another. I shall not kill him, but I shall hand him over. We shall take him first to Tiree, for on no account must we allow him to see our plans in Rannoch. Then everything is easy. A boat from Tiree to the Solway—a day's sail and there we are."

While the masked leader was thus ruminating, Rob Roy, eager and alert, but unconscious of immediate danger, entered the glen.

In the growing darkness Rob Roy's keen eye swept over all the likely places in which an enemy might be concealed, and he pushed forward with all speed so that he might clear the glen before absolute darkness set in.

He knew the glen was a short one, but he could not be expected to know that the masked leader had crept silently behind the thick bushes of broom, and was waiting with a murderous stone in his hand to hurl it at the Highland chieftain the moment he passed.

Immediately Rob Roy came level with the deep fringe of furze and broom bushes, the masked leader hurled the stone with terrific force, striking Rob Roy, as the thrower intended, fair and square on the chest.

Rob Roy staggered back under the impact, and fell to the ground in a semi-conscious condition, and gasping for breath.

" Now I have you," exclaimed the masked leader, triumphantly, as he sprang on the prostrate Highland Chieftain and firmly bound his hands behind his back. " Now I have you. A price is on your head. And, you will lose it for tampering with the retainers of the Wolf of Rannoch."

As yet Rob Roy could not speak, but

as he looked his captor up and down, he observed that on the mask above his forehead was the representation of a white wolf.

"To whom have I the honour?" asked Rob Roy, composedly, when he had regained his breath and raised himself to a sitting position.

"You are a prisoner of the Wolf of Rannoch," replied the masked leader.

"And who may he be when he is at home?" asked Rob Roy, sarcastically. "If he be like you, he is a coward who is also ashamed to show his face."

"Beware, Rob Roy," exclaimed the other fiercely. "Tempt me not too much. Your life is forfeit for entering the territory of the Wolf of Rannoch, but I have preserved you for a certain reason. There is a £1,000 reward for your capture, and for that I have spared you."

"At least you are candid," replied Rob Roy. "But pray, who is the Wolf of Rannoch. I am a neighbour, as one might say, and I should like to make his acquaintance."

"That you cannot do," replied the man. "The Wolf you will never see; but I am his representative, and no man dare enter the lands he has made his own."

"Made his own," exclaimed Rob Roy. "This is something new, and I'll warrant you the MacGregors will have much pleasure in paying the Wolf a domiciliary visit."

"Without their chief," laughed the leader, grimly.

"It matters not," replied Rob Roy, calmly. "What do you intend doing now?"

"To hand you over to justice."

"To justice," retorted Rob Roy in disgust. "To justice. Why, man, a common cut-throat like you talking of handing a man over to justice."

"There is a price on your head."

"You said so before. I shall be pleased to go with you now."

"Not so fast, my proud Highland chieftain, and kindly keep your tongue within bounds, if you wish to be well looked after. If not, I shall thrust you in one of the lowest dungeons of the stronghold."

"A stronghold," ejaculated Rob Roy. "I am learning something new every minute! Then you have a stronghold in this vicinity."

The robber bit his lips. He saw he had said too much.

"'Tis but a figure of speech," he said. "The stronghold that will keep you is but a mud-hut a few yards away."

The masked leader whistled shrilly three times, and immediately the sound of footsteps came from the distance. In a few minutes four masked men appeared, but as darkness had now set in, Rob Roy could hardly distinguish them.

"Lead him to the hut," said the leader, "keep strict guard over him, and at daylight you shall receive your orders."

Rob Roy was led to the hut. It was a small building of two rooms, and when a fir candle was lighted Rob Roy saw that it contained a bed, a table, and a chair, with a few dishes arranged on a dresser by the wall.

"'Tis chilly to-night," said one of the men, as he arranged a wood fire in the open fireplace and lit it.

Rob Roy watched his gaolers intently, but all attempts on his part to open up a conversation were foiled.

"The best thing you can do," growled one of the men, "is to lie on the bed, for doubtless in the morning you may have a journey."

As nothing was to be gained in attempting to change the resolution of the men, Rob Roy lay down and pretended to sleep, although sleep was as far removed from him as his beloved Loch Ard.

He determined to escape, and revolved plans in his brain. But escape seemed impossible, for two of the men deliberately strewed sweet smelling heather for a bed at the foot of the door and placidly lay down, effectually barring an exit. The other two men took up positions on either side of the fireplace. Thus the only means of escape were closed.

Through his half-closed eyes Rob Roy watched them. They were all tall, powerful men, and dressed alike in rough, home-spun hunting shirts, and trousers of the same material bound to their legs with thongs made of the skin of the red deer. They were, also, armed to the teeth.

Presently one of the men at the fire took a sand-glass from the cupboard. It was shaped something after the style of a double syphon with the top globe filled with sand. As the man stood it on end, the sand began to filter through in a very thin stream to the lower globe.

"It is a two-hour sand-glass," muttered Rob Roy, "and when the sand has run out they will waken the men at the door for their turn to watch."

The hours passed slowly, and as Rob Roy had guessed, the men at the door were aroused when the sand had run its time, while the watchers flung themselves on the heather. The new sentries immediately reversed the glass, when the sands of time began to run once more.

The night seemed interminable. Rob Roy tossed about on his bed as the watchers kept their silent vigil.

Soon daylight began to appear. In a few seconds there was a sound of horses' hoofs on the hard ground, followed by a thundering knock at the door.

The men sprang to their feet instantly, and through the door stalked the leader of the masked patrol.

"So," he exclaimed in an attempt at jocularity, "we have still our little red bird safe."

"In the safe keeping of the black hawks of the hills," replied Rob Roy, fearlessly. "Nothing much escapes a hooded crow."

The leader's smile changed to a scowl.

"Have less to say," he thundered. "Make him some breakfast," he added to the men, "for he has a long journey in front of him.

Some smoked red deer was quickly cooked, and after breakfast Rob Roy was ordered to mount one of the horses standing tethered outside the door.

With his hands tied behind his back he was lifted on horseback, and his feet firmly secured by a rope passing beneath the horse's stomach.

Calling to his men, who instantly mounted, the cavalcade set off. Turning their backs to the sun, they rode at a smart canter, and Rob Roy knew that they were travelling due west.

They did not draw rein until they came to the shores of Loch Leven, the leader meanwhile going on in front.

In a short time he galloped back. "The lugger is at the landing-place," he exclaimed. "Trot."

In a few minutes they arrived at "the landing-place," which was merely a natural inlet in the water. A small boat was waiting for them, and soon they were hauled on board the lugger.

Rob Roy was at once conducted down below to the captain's cabin.

"I have heard of your prowess as a swimmer," said the leader of the masked patrol, "so you will be kept safely in the captain's cabin. In the meantime, adieu, I might say farewell for ever, for we shall never meet." And the masked leader turned on his heel and clambered upstairs.

"There's many a slip," exclaimed Rob Roy after him, but the leader had reached the deck, and he and his men rowed ashore in the small boat.

Rob Roy glanced about the cabin, and rose with the intention of running up the steep steps, when he was startled by a hoarse voice in the cabin.

From the dark end of the cabin, from whence the voice came, Rob Roy could see the glint of a pistol pointed straight at him.

"Ha, ha!" said the voice; "we are prepared for all emergencies. If you move you are a dead man."

Rob Roy peered into the darkness, and as his eyes grew accustomed to the place he discerned a masked man lying on his stomach on a bunk below the ladder, and pointing a pistol at his breast.

"Better sit down," grumbled the man, "and make the best of a bad job. I am responsible for you until our journey's end."

"And where might that be?" asked Rob Roy.

"To where the Wolf of Rannoch has ordered."

"That is not much information, my man," said Rob Roy.

"As much as I intend to give," was the gruff reply. "Take my advice, and make yourself comfortable. If you attempt to escape I shall shoot you dead."

And nothing further would the man say. No blandishment or entreaty on Rob Roy's part could draw from him another syllable. All that Rob Roy saw was the cold glint of the muzzle of the pistol as it projected above the woodwork of the bunk.

In a few minutes the lugger cast anchor and began to move.

"I shall soon be able to tell," thought Rob Roy, "if we are on the open sea; but I expect the lugger will crawl along Loch Leven, into Loch Linnhe, through the sound of Mull, and onwards to Tiree. No better hiding place could be got than this westermost isle. And it is said the vessels losing their way at sea, always get washed up against the island, hence, no doubt, the reason of the abode there of those wreckers and ruffians."

A weary day passed, and at last the man spoke.

" Better lie down in a bunk. We have a long journey."

" A slow lugger," thought Rob Roy, as he took the man's advice and lay down. Hardly had his head touched the pillow than he was fast asleep.

CHAPTER IV.

A PERILOUS JOURNEY.

Rob Roy was awakened by the scud of hurrying feet on the deck above, and the hoarse orders of the captain. He gazed about him in wonder, but quickly remembered the predicament he was in.

" Rouse yourself," said his gaoler. " We shall be going ashore in a minute."

Rob Roy gladly crawled from his bunk. His arms were aching with the tightening cords.

" Loosen these bonds a little," he asked the man.

" Catch a weasel asleep," replied the man with a harsh laugh. " No. Shut your eyes, for I am going to blindfold you."

It was a bitter disappointment to Rob Roy, for he had been thinking of escape. But there was nothing for it but to obey. He was led to the deck, and the fresh sea breezes blew on his cheeks.

" Give me your hand "—it was the gaoler who spoke—" and be careful of your footing. We are crossing a plank to the quay."

Rob Roy felt the plank give below his weight, but in a minute he stood on firm ground.

From the noises he knew that there were many men about, and soon the order was given to advance. For some minutes they moved forward over rocky ground.

" Take off the bandage," said a voice in authority. " Undo the bonds on his arms."

Rob Roy looked about him. He was in a valley surrounded by hills. In front of him stood a tall, powerful, bearded man with one eye, and all around him were armed men. Their

dress showed their trade—thick guernseys, sea-boots and cutlasses.

Rob Roy looked the leader straight in the face.

" You are known as Peter," said Rob Roy.

" Ha! You know me? You are Rob Roy, and in a few days time we take another journey."

" Sufficient to the day is the evil thereof," replied Rob Roy. " At present I am hungry."

" Oh, we shall attend to you all right," laughed Peter of the one eye. " Bring the ponies," he ordered to the men.

" Mount," he said to Rob Roy, as a small, sturdy Highland pony was led to his side.

" I prefer to walk," said Rob Roy.

Peter laughed. " Take my advice," he said meaningly, " and mount. You will require it. You will see by-and-by. At least my men with their bumble feet need them."

The men laughed loudly. " It must be a funny joke," muttered Rob Roy to himself, " although I can't see it at present."

The cavalcade rode towards the mountains, and soon began to thread its way along a bridle path that led to a narrow pathway that seemed to hang between heaven and earth.

It was cut deep into the mountain side, and as it skirted the sheer mass of perpendicular rock that withstood the fierce blasts from the sea it gradually narrowed as the ascent proceeded.

Peter led the way, Rob Roy came next, with the remainder of the band in rear.

Hundreds of feet below the sea roared in the rocks where men clambering about looked like pigmies.

" Whew," whistled Rob Roy softly to himself as the pathway became so narrow that it did not look wide enough to allow one pony to pass, " I prefer to be on my feet. This may be good enough for those bumble-footed wreckers, but it is not good enough for a Highlander."

The men relied entirely on the sure-footed Highland ponies that picked their way along the edge of the dizzy cliff with the utmost *sang froid*.

" Do as I do," shouted Peter when they came to an exceedingly narrow path. Flinging his left leg over the saddle, Peter sat his pony like a lady, with his feet dangling over the edge of the precipice. The manœuvre was at once apparent, for the pathway admitted the body of the ponies only, while the sagacious animals hugged the side of the stupendous rocks as closely as they could.

"This is not good enough for me," exclaimed Rob Roy, and in a second he slid from the pony's back, and with one quick movement placed himself in front of it.

The men behind, together with Peter in front, stared at Rob Roy in amazement at his perilous feat.

"This tomfoolery may be good enough for sea-robbers, but it is child's play to a mountaineer born and bred."

No answer was returned, for the men were too preoccupied with their dangerous journey. None of them dare look below, for the slightest swerving would have hurled them to instant death.

Rob Roy led his pony quite unconcerned. "I shall have to keep a sharp look-out for that fellow," muttered one-eyed Peter.

As he spoke the path suddenly broadened, and veering to the left led into a cavern of large dimensions.

The savoury smell of cooking was wafted to Rob Roy's nostrils, and at once he observed that the outer part of the cavern was used as a kitchen, at which one man, also in large sea boots, was busily engaged over several steaming pots.

The men dismounted at the entrance to the cavern, and each hobbled his pony, and allowed it to graze on the grass of the plateau.

The inner cavern was lighted by one or two lamps, and as Rob Roy's eyes grew accustomed to the darkness he saw that the walls were hung with cutlasses and pistols. At the further end were boxes of ship's stores, all stolen from vessels either wrecked or lured to the inhospitable coast.

"Make yourself at home," said Peter, waving his hand around the cave. "And now let us have something to eat."

CHAPTER V.

A CATASTROPHE.

They had just finished dinner when suddenly two reports of a gun in rapid succession made the men in the cave spring to their feet.

"The lugger from the mainland," they exclaimed in one breath and ran for their ponies.

"Deverell," shouted Peter above the din, "wait behind and guard the prisoner, and in a moment the wreckers had mounted their ponies and were cautiously moving along the bridle path.

Deverell waited until they were out of sight. "The prisoner is safe enough," he muttered. "I'm not going to lose my chance of the pick of things from the lugger, so here goes."

Without casting a look at Rob Roy, he mounted his pony and followed the others.

Rob Roy sprang to his feet. Daylight streaming through the entrance showed him that even the cook had left in the hurry to meet the incoming lugger.

In a moment Rob Roy seized a cutlass and was moving swiftly along the path. At the first bend he almost overtook the man with whom he was left in charge, so he slowed his pace, and reached the valley in safety.

Making for the nearest hill because it was covered with thick bushes, Rob Roy concealed himself, but remembering that he had better make sure of his exact position before nightfall, he proceeded to climb the hill cautiously.

When he gained the crest, he drew back suddenly at the hum of voices. Only a few feet below him were the wreckers grouped together. Peering through the bushes he saw them plainly.

They were talking excitedly, and all at once, and no wonder, for out in the bay volumes of smoke and flame were rising from a vessel.

"The powder magazine has blown up," cried one.

"The oil tank has taken fire," exclaimed another.

"The tar for the night flares has done the damage," shouted a third.

"Keep silence!" shouted One-eyed Peter. "Send the boats from the harbour at once."

Several of the men scampered down the mountain-path towards the harbour to carry out the order.

But in the meantime the crew of the lugger had lowered a boat, and were pulling towards the shore.

When One-eyed Peter saw this he ran

towards the harbour. In a few minutes the lugger's crew pulled ashore.

"What about the boy?" demanded Peter of the captain of the lugger. "Did you manage it all right?"

"To tell you the truth, he's done for. The second day out during a squall we missed him. Fell overboard, I expect," laughed the captain, a hard, scowling-faced man. "In any case it saved us the trouble."

"Humph," muttered Peter. "What about the lugger?"

"Just as we were rounding the bay the fore hatch burst into flames. The oil and the night flares caught fire somehow, and we could do nothing to save the powder magazine. To save ourselves we took to the boat. There she goes."

As he spoke a roar of thunder shook the bay, while a mass of flame shot high in the heavens. In a moment nothing was left of the lugger but a mass of floating wreckage.

"That's bad luck," growled Peter.

"Worse luck if we had been in it," returned the captain.

"Humph!—any message?"

"Yes," replied the captain. "This letter, which has to be forwarded without delay to Rannoch."

Peter took the letter and read the address. "Urgent. To Harpour, Rannoch."

"All right," he said, as he glanced swiftly towards the sea. "'Tis no good looking at broken spars. Let us to the cave and discuss what is to be done."

CHAPTER VI.

A DARING DEED.

Rob Roy witnessed the destruction of the lugger, but before the final scene his quick eye detected a black object bobbing about in the sea.

"It is a human being," he muttered, as he concentrated his gaze on the object. "Those inhuman wretches in the hurry to save themselves have left one of their companions behind."

Rob Roy's attention was at once centred in the unfortunate man, for he decided that the object that had attracted his attention was a man, although he could only make out a movement of the object now and then.

Rob Roy's generous heart swelled within him, and, as was his wont, he

determined to rescue the unfortunate man at all costs.

The bay stretched in a semi-circle, and he observed that the sea, rushing towards the headland on the right, created an extremely swift current that dashed itself against the rocks that, jutting out into the bay, formed a natural breakwater.

Once in that current no vessel could live, not to mention a human being, and Rob Roy saw that the castaway was gradually nearing the spot when he should be sucked into the vortex.

Without hesitation, and not counting for a moment the personal risk he ran in being recaptured, Rob Roy quickly descended the hill, and running the gauntlet of the valley, rapidly passed behind the town.

Swiftly he skirted the rocky bay, and just as the castaway was drawn into the current, he darted over the slippery rocks, and plunged into the raging sea.

Powerful swimmer that he was, Rob Roy could do nothing except barely hold his own against the tide. But he had prepared for that emergency with true Highland sagacity, and had jumped into the water at a point where the castaway would be swept past before being hurled to death on the rocks.

With superhuman efforts he maintained his position on the fringe of the current, and as he rose and fell with the waves he kept his eagle eye on the castaway.

In a moment the man was sucked into the vortex, and was being carried straight for the rocks.

With the velocity of lightning he was dragged under water and shot past Rob Roy.

But Rob Roy had been saving his strength for the final effort. If he failed death would be his portion.

His keen eye detected the dark spot in the water a few yards to the right, and like a flash he dived below the rushing water.

Almost at the same minute he appeared twenty yards away with the unconscious castaway in his arms and struck boldly out to sea.

With innate cunning he had cleared the deadly narrow current. Gallantly he battled with the waves and turned his face towards the headland on the right. Well he knew that to attempt to cross the current in the bay was to court death.

Keeping to the open sea, Rob Roy reached a point opposite the headland against which the sea dashed with fury, and created the dangerous current.

Treading water for a few seconds, Rob Roy took his bearings and struck out for the further side of the headland, where he saw a narrow strip of sand.

Clearing the head of the current, and floating the man in front of him, Rob Roy allowed the breakers to carry him landward, and at the proper moment, when his feet touched ground, he seized his burden, and sprang forward, clearing the receding wave.

Struggling to the beach, he placed the castaway gently on the sand and gasped for breath.

"By heavens," he panted, "it is a boy!"

In a few seconds he regained his breath and commenced to resuscitate the boy.

Making a pillow of his wet clothes, Rob Roy rubbed and pummelled the boy incessantly.

"Ah!" he exclaimed, as the boy showed signs of reviving. "Now he will soon be all right."

"Where am I?" moaned the boy.

"With a friend," replied Rob Roy, as he rubbed more and more.

In a short time the boy was able to sit up. He looked around abstractedly. "Where am I?" again he asked.

"All right, my boy," replied Rob Roy, encouragingly. "You'll soon be all right."

"Am I safe from the pirates?" he asked.

"Don't be alarmed, my boy. Rob Roy will protect you."

"Oh!" exclaimed the boy. "Are you Rob Roy? I have heard a lot about you in Cumberland."

"You come from Cumberland, then?" asked Rob Roy.

"Yes," replied the boy. "My father is Lord Rowelpeak. I am his son Ulric."

"Then," said Rob Roy, "you are Lord Ulric of Hazelheath. Why I know your father. Do you know that I was the one who chose the Highland cattle that he is so proud of in his park?"

"I did not know that," replied Ulric; "but I do know that they are very fine animals. But how are you here, wherever that may be. Are we in Scotland?"

"Yes. In part of it, i believe. In the island of Tiree, but let us hide amongst the bushes while our clothes dry. I have a story to tell and no doubt you have one.

CHAPTER VII.
THE ESCAPE.

When the wreckers returned to the cave and found that Rob Roy had escaped, their rage knew no bounds. Luckily for him, while he was rescuing the boy, the whole of the wreckers had returned to the cave to hear the story of the burning of the lugger, and so they had not witnessed his daring deed.

By the time they had again descended the valley, Rob Roy had safely landed beyond the promontory, out of sight of the look-out, and when they commenced to search the island Rob Roy and Ulric were quietly ensconced in a hiding-place chosen by Rob Roy.

While the wreckers were scouring the island, Rob Roy was listening to Ulric's story.

"We have been very unlucky lately," he was saying. "Only last week my sister disappeared most mysteriously, and here am I as the result of a fishing expedition."

"Your sister missing? You don't mean Lady Clare, the great Cumberland beauty, whom I met with your father?" exclaimed Rob Roy.

"I have only one sister, and last week she disappeared most mysteriously, and only two days ago a friend of my father persuaded me, much against my will, to go a fishing expedition with him. He said it would take my mind away from our trouble, and here I am."

"But how? I don't understand." said Rob Roy.

"Well," replied Ulric, "we went fishing in the Solway and almost within sight of land we were attacked by pirates. My friend, or rather my father's friend, defended us most gallantly until he was stunned by a blow. I was taken on board the lugger, although I fought for all I was worth. But a fellow can't do much with a pistol at his ear all the time."

"And your friend?"

"I never saw him again. I was sent below at once, and next day, when I asked what had become of him, they told me he was dead."

"What is your friend's name?"

"Renshaw. He is a landed proprietor in the neighbourhood. He is very sweet on Clare, but she does not care for him. He was terribly cut up at her mysterious disappearance, and swore that he would find her. He engaged a special post-chaise to go to London and bring back the best detectives they have in the capital."

"And what happened to you after you were told he was dead?"

"I had a terrible time, for I overheard a conversation between the captain and the mate when they thought I was asleep. I heard the mate say, 'What do you intend doing with the youngster?' and the captain added, 'The orders are to heave him overboard at the first opportunity. I could have cracked his skull at the capture, but he fought so gamely I hadn't it in me to give him his *congé*. However, it's got to be done. You know in the North Channel, with a bit of a sea on, man overboard is a common occurrence.'"

"My blood ran cold," continued Ulric, "and I determined to hide on the first possible occasion. So during the second day at sea, when a squall struck the vessel, I hid in the fore hatch. I kept in the stifling place, for I don't know how long. It seemed an eternity, and although I could smell oil I determined to strike a light. I had a flint and some touch paper in my pocket, but when I ignited the paper it burned my fingers, and I involuntarily cast it from me. In a moment the hold was in a blaze. I don't know how I got out, but I saw the crew take to the only boat, while I jumped over the other side, clinging to a spar that I found on the deck. Then I knew nothing more until I found myself with you."

Rob Roy then told him his story.

"But the girl," said the boy.

"I believe," replied Rob Roy, "she is your sister. There is some terrible mystery about this, but by heaven it shall be cleared up."

"They will be scouring the island, so we must remain here quite quiet until night, then we shall seize a boat and escape. You see from here, if you peer through the bottom of the bushes, we can discern at once from all sides if any one approaches."

"It is well chosen," whispered the boy.

"They will never think of looking here. It is so easily seen, this green patch on the hill-top. They will look in all the likely places, in the caves, in the valleys, and amongst the rocks. At least for one day we are safe."

It was as Rob Roy said. The wreckers searched high and low, but never dreamt of looking at the low-lying bushes that crowned the hill overlooking the very harbour.

When night came, Rob Roy whispered to Ulric to keep perfectly still while he crept out and reconnoitred.

Making his way cautiously to the harbour—a rough-and-ready roadstead of rough planks—he heard the sound of voices.

"Why don't you light your lamp?" exclaimed a voice.

"I am just doing it," grumbled another voice, "if you'll only give me time."

"Well, hurry up. The yawl has to sail to-night."

"What's that for. They are in a desperate hurry all at once."

"I can't help that. An important letter is being carried by no other than Peter. It is on urgent business, and he has to see Harpour."

"Drat them, I say."

"Never mind that. Hurry up. Peter is waiting, and I have to tell him when the boat is ready."

After lots of mutual grumbling the two men made up their minds that the yawl was ready, and one of them started off to inform One-eyed Peter of that fact.

Rob Roy made up his mind in an instant, and shrank back into the shadows.

As the man passed him, he sprang on him like a leopard, clapping his hand over his mouth. In Rob Roy's herculean grasp, the man was like clay in the potter's hand.

In a moment Rob Roy gagged him with a piece of his plaid, and ripping a long strip from the same material, securely bound his arms and legs. Carrying him away from the footpath he laid the man down on the heather.

In a moment he sprang on board the yawl, and before the frightened occupant could call out, he gagged and bound him in turn with material he found in the cabin. Quickly he carried him ashore, and placed him beside the other man. Returning to the yawl, he found rope eminently suited to his purpose, also more cloth. In a few minutes he bound the two men back to back, and placed an extra piece of cloth round their mouths to prevent any chance of their being heard.

Hardly had he done this than a harsh voice sounded close at hand. It was One-eyed Peter.

"How now? What is the meaning of this? Haven't you got that yawl ready yet—ough!"

Rob Roy sprang on him and felled him with a blow. One-eyed Peter lay as one dead.

"It is not a method I like or approve," muttered Rob Roy, as he passed his hands rapidly over Peter's body, but necessity knows no law."

"I'll take this," continued Rob Roy, as he helped himself to Peter's pistols and his sword. "They will come handy. And I'll help myself to this," and he took the letter from Peter's breast. "Ah! This, then, is the important letter. At least we shall see."

Rapidly he made for the hiding-place,

"Hist," he whispered. "Are you there?"

"Yes," replied Ulric. "I thought something had happened to you."

"I have been long, but many things have happened. Quick, come along!"

The two quickly made their way on board the yawl, and in a very short time they pushed off.

"We shall steer due east," said Rob Roy, "and we must strike either Ulva, Staffa, or Mull, at any rate."

As it happened in the darkness Rob Roy turned the bow of the yawl direct north-east, and by the early morning they found themselves sailing up a land-locked piece of water.

"We are near land, anyway," said Ulric with a laugh.

"Yes," replied Rob Roy, smilingly, "and once on land we are free."

As he spoke a fishing boat hove in sight.

Rob Roy hailed it in Gaelic.

"Where are we?" he asked.

"In Loch Sunart," was the relpy.

Rob Roy lifted his bonnet and shouted thanks. "We are in luck," he said, turning to Lord Ulric. "This leads to Strontian, and from Strontian over the hills is but a stone's throw from Loch Linnhe, so to speak, and we can land at Ballachulish. From there I know every inch of the ground to home."

"And home you must come with

me," continued Rob Roy, "and then I shall escort you home to Cumberland. What part of Cumberland? Maryport, if I remember rightly."

"Yes. That is right. Just a few miles from Maryport."

"Good," replied Rob Roy. "Then we shall sail straight on to the end of the loch to Strontian."

CHAPTER VIII.
Breaking the News.

It was as Rob Roy said. The yawl arrived at the end of the loch safely, and leaving the boat in charge of some fishermen, Rob Roy and Ulric struck across country.

At the shores of Loch Linnhe they found kind-hearted fishermen who gladly conveyed them to Ballachulish.

At Ballachulish, where Rob Roy was known, he was received with delight.

"Your brother, Alastair," said the village shipwright, "has been scouring the whole country for you. He lost you, he says, and he tracked you to the loch. He has been inquiring high and low if any one has seen you."

"It is time, then," replied Rob Roy, after he had thanked the people, "that we pushed forward."

The journey overland to Loch Ard was soon accomplished, and Rob Roy had a right royal welcome from his wife and his people. But he had made up his mind to probe the mystery to the bottom, so the following day he and Ulric set off for Glasgow.

At Glasgow they joined the stage for Carlisle, and from thence journeyed to Maryport.

Arrived at Rowelpeak Castle, Lord Ulric blew a long blast on the horn at the drawbridge. Instantly the wicket gate on the other side of the moat opened, and when the seneschal saw Lord Ulric he staggered back.

"Lord Ulric," he exclaimed, "are you really in the flesh? You are mourned for as dead. Your mother is in bed with the shock, and your father's hair has turned grey. Are you really in the flesh?"

"Let down the drawbridge, quick!" ordered Lord Ulric; "quick, good Preston. I am as much in the flesh as ever I was."

The drawbridge was let down, and

Ulrich and Rob Roy crossed over with celerity.

"What is this you were saying?" demanded Lord Ulric.

"My lord," replied the seneschal, "come into the guard-house, for too great a shock to your noble parents might be fatal."

"But what is it all about?" asked Ulric.

"It is this," replied the seneschal. "When you went fishing with Mr. Renshaw, he returned that night, sorely bruised it is true, with the tale that you had been attacked by the Solway pirates, that you had been killed, and that he had had a marvellous escape."

"Tell me the story in detail," eagerly asked Lord Ulric.

"He said, my lord, that when you were in the boat the pirates attacked you; that he fought as well as he could; that he was knocked on the head, and that when he recovered he found himself on board a pirate lugger; that he lay as if insensible for some time; that he heard them say that you were dead, and that at the first opportunity he crawled to the side and slipped overboard unperceived."

"Why, they told me he was dead!" exclaimed Lord Ulric.

"But how did he get ashore?" asked Rob Roy, who had been an interested listener.

"He said, sir, that when he slipped overboard he swam for some time, and luckily encountered the boat in which he had been fishing. With superhuman efforts he scrambled on board and made for land."

"And where is Renshaw?" asked Lord Ulric.

"He left two days ago in quest of the Lady Clare, in company with some clever men from London."

"And what did the London men say?" asked Lord Ulric.

"They said nothing," was the reply, "but one of them muttered that there was something wrong somewhere."

"A very wise remark," said Lord Ulric.

"But how are we to break the news?" asked the seneschal.

"I can manage that," interposed Rob Roy. "Some years ago I met Lord Rowelpeak and we formed, I believe, a mutual admiration for each other. I can break the news gently."

"A good idea," said the seneschal. "My lord will remain here while I conduct your friend to Lord Rowelpeak."

"Rob Roy MacGregor," said Rob Roy, bowing.

The seneschal bowed.

Rob Roy was ushered into Lord Rowelpeak's private room. The old earl scarcely looked up. His head was resting on his arm on the table.

But the red tartan and noble bearing of the MacGregor were objects to arrest anyone's attention at all times.

"What," exclaimed Lord Rowelpeak, rising to his feet and holding out his hand, "surely not the noble MacGregor?"

"Your servant, sir," replied Rob Roy, with dignity. "I hope—indeed I am sure I do not intrude on your privacy at the present moment."

"You do not, MacGregor. Although my heart is broken. Of course you have heard?"

"I have," replied Rob Roy. "And that very reason brings me from Scotland."

Lord Rowelpeak sat bolt upright and gazed intently at the fearless eyes of the Highland chieftain, as if to fathom their depths, looking for a ray of hope.

"MacGregor," he said, slowly, without relinquishing his gaze, "you and I belong to different countries, although we are of the same people. You are a noble of the Highlands, I of the lowlands. I ask you as a nobleman, is there any hope?"

"And I answer, my lord, there is. There is hope out of your trouble."

"I know," said Lord Rowelpeak, with painful slowness as if speaking to himself—"I know a MacGregor would never lie, but this is too much. I dread—oh,' MacGregor!—I dread that fate may mock me."

"Fate shall not mock you," replied Rob Roy, swiftly. "Not if I have anything to do with it."

"And what have you to do with it?" asked Lord Rowelpeak, trying to master his emotion.

"My lord," replied Rob Roy. "I am not here to embitter your sorrow. I am here to relieve it. Since I saw you last you have aged by twenty years. I have good news. Are you calm?"

"My daughter?"

"No; your son and heir. You asked me what I had to do with it. I say everything."

" You have seen him ? "

" Yes. Listen. Now, be calm. I know where he is."

" I am calm, MacGregor. You do not mock me."

" Lord Rowelpeak," replied Rob Roy, advancing to his side and whispering, " I can bring him to your presence."

" When ? "

" Now. He is in the castle."

At that moment the door flew open, and Lord Ulric rushed into the room.

" Father," he called, " you have been talking such a long time that I had to break the strain. You must thank the noble MacGregor for my life."

The stately Lord Rowelpeak rose and grasped Rob Roy's hand.

" I knew it, MacGregor, when you you appeared," he said, hoarsely, " that you were the bearer of good news, but I have had so many shocks of late that I have steeled my soul against surprises, good or evil."

" You have been hard hit, Lord Rowelpeak," replied Rob Roy, " but everything may come right. The Lady Clare may yet be safe."

" Ah, yes, my good friend, Renshaw is moving heaven and earth. He loves her. He has asked for my consent. I have said if she loves him. But he is going to find her. He is certain."

" What is that, my lord ? "

" Well, it looks like a confession of weakness, but as matter of fact, three days ago, he had such a curious dream. He dreamt the same thing three times in succession."

" What was the dream ? "

" That she had been kidnapped by an adventurer, and that she had been carried away to a retreat amongst mountains. He described this place as it appeared in his dream. It was a strongly-built castle far removed from habitation in the vicinity of water. On one side this water was bounded by a huge mountain chain, while on the other side of the water the ground was flat, but in the distance towered a noble mountain."

" And has he any idea where this place is ? " asked Rob Roy.

" None whatever. But he is a believer in dreams, and says that the spirit will lead him. He has started."

" In which direction did he go ? "

" I cannot tell. All I know is that two days ago, after a conference with the men he brought from London, he said he felt he would be successful."

" I hope so," replied Rob Roy, " although I have no belief in those old women's theories."

CHAPTER IX.
FORBIDDING THE BANNS.

When the story was bruited abroad of how Rob Roy had saved the heir of Rowelpeak he was treated with marked respect by everyone in the castle.

Lady Rowelpeak recovered rapidly, and she never tired talking of the prowess of Rob Roy.

" If ever my daughter is restored to us," she declared, " it will be through that noble chieftain of the MacGregors.

Rob Roy was pressed to stay at the Castle, and the only thing that induced him to do so was the fact that, in Mr. Renshaw's dream, Lady Clare was to be restored within four days.

Although he disclaimed all belief in dreams, Rob Roy hoped against hope that the dream might come true. At the same time his real reason for staying was that he wished to see the gentlemen who had interested himself so much in Lord Rowelpeak's family.

On the following morning the castle was in a state of turmoil. Shortly after the break of day Mr. Renshaw had arrived and with him Lady Clare. Never was there such rejoicings, and Clare poured out her story to her mother.

After the ball, when she was waiting for her carriage, a vehicle drove up very like her own. It was announced as that of the Lady Clare of Rowelpeak. She jumped in and instantly she was gagged. For several days she travelled in this carriage with changes of horses, and at last when they came in a wild part of the country a horseman, masked and ungainly, seized her and carried her away.

For a day or two she had to remain in a comparatively newly-built house until at last there was terrible uproar, and Mr. Renshaw, sword in hand, rushed into the room and rescued her. She never liked him until that moment. She did not love him, but she respected a man who had risked his life for her.

" Well, my love," said her mother, " you must choose for yourself—if you love him, have him."

" But I do not love him, mother.

Only he is so pressing. I respect him, but——"

" But what, my dear ? "

" I do not love him."

In the castle Rob Roy was eclipsed. The romantic ending of Mr. Renshaw's dream and his daring deeds in bringing it to a conclusion appealed to all.

Mr. Renshaw was the hero, and when the Lady Clare heard his praises on all sides her heart relented. She began to think that her own opinion might be wrong, and at last she consented to become his wife.

Great preparations were made for the marriage ceremony, and Lord Rowelpeak pressed Rob Roy to stay.

" It is only another seven days, you know, that we must keep you from your home," he said, jocularly.

" I am only too pleased," replied Rob Roy, " to be a honoured guest, although I would prefer naturally to be in my own home."

Mr. Renshaw was a striking-looking man. He was tall, had a strong face, and was very pleasant. His hair was beginning to be tinged with grey, and, of course, was much older than the Lady Clare, who had just turned nineteen.

What Rob Roy thought of him no one could tell, for he could not be drawn into a conversation about him. All he would say was, " He is a friend of Lord Rowelpeak, and Lord Rowelpeak is a friend of mine."

The Lady Clare, one of the most beautiful women in England at the time, looked weighed down with woe, instead of a happy girl going to be married.

Rob Roy saw her several times, and muttered to himself.

" If what I think is true," he repeated to himself, " I am justified, but if I am wrong I shall do a great injury. I can think better when I am among my own people."

This thought preyed on his mind, and Rob Roy could not sleep. So one night, when all had retired to rest, he wandered through the corridors of the castle, and mounting the old stone stairs sought refuge amidst the breezes of the night on the roof.

He was thinking deeply when he was startled by the sound of voices ascending the stairs. Unconsciously he drew back in the shadows, and immediately two figures appeared. They were whispering to each other so softly that Rob Roy could not hear.

" Everything is all right," he heard one voice say, and he recognised the speaker as Mr. Renshaw. " You had better wait for the marriage."

Rob Roy could not hear the answer, but he stared hard at the speaker.

" But the letter ? " said Renshaw.

" It was taken from me by Rob Roy."

" He is in the castle."

" Then let us murder him to-night. Which room is his ? "

" The guest room."

Rob Roy nearly burst out laughing. He recognised the second whisperer. It was One-eyed Peter.

" A nice game these precious scoundrels are playing," he muttered.

" No," whispered Renshaw, " do not let him think we suspect him. Let the marriage pass. Then you can do as you like. As you know, my money is about expended, but after my marriage with the Lady Clare I can give you what you like."

" It is as I thought," muttered Rob Roy. " Lord Rowelpeak, rich though he be, is in the hands of sharpers."

" Well, I want to get to bed," said Renshaw.

" And I can do with the same," whispered One-eyed Peter. " When the marriage is over I can settle the account."

With that they disappeared below.

On the following morning the Castle was *en fête*, and at the appointed time the bride, Lord Rowelpeak, the bridegroom, and the best man were at their places at the altar in the private chapel.

The clergyman intoned the service, and as he was about to tie the nuptial knot, he said, " If any man hath——"

" I have," thundered Rob Roy from the body of the chapel, " I forbid the banns."

There was a dead silence for a moment that seemed an eternity.

" State your cause in the vestry," said the clergyman.

" I can state it now. This Mr. Renshaw is the husband of many women ; he is a retired pirate of the West Indian Islands ; his name is Twaite, and he is known as the Wolf of Rannoch, the robber, the oppressor of the poor. If you do not believe me, ask the one-eyed retainer of the house of Renshaw —*alias* the pirate and wrecker of the island of Tiree. In proof of my statement I hold in my hand a letter from this same Renshaw to one Harpour of Rannoch, per One-eyed Peter, the retainer."

At the first sound of the voice the bride turned ghastly white, and when the full explanation came she fell fainting on the floor.

Renshaw turned round fiercely. "This is infamous," he cried, "and by one of my father-in-law's guests, too, a wild Highlander."

The scene in the chapel was one of the utmost confusion. The bridesmaids carried the fainting bride away, while the clergyman tried to assuage the commotion Rob Roy has caused.

"We shall adjourn to the vestry," he said, motioning Rob Roy to come forward.

As Rob Roy advanced, Lord Rowelpeak met him. "What tomfoolery is this?" he exclaimed, his eyes flashing with anger. "Have I not had enough trouble?"

"Yes," replied Rob Roy, "and had it not been for me you would have been in worse trouble."

"Not so, MacGregor, clever as you are, you have made a terrible mistake this time."

"And I tell you," retorted MacGregor, "you have made the mistake. However, I am answerable to the clergyman, not to you."

When Rob Roy reached the vestry, the clergyman, along with the bridegroom, was awaiting him. Lord Rowelpeak followed.

"What means this terrible mistake," exclaimed Mr. Renshaw, dramatically.

Rob Roy met his gaze without flinching.

"There is no mistake, Twaite," replied Rob Roy. "I refuse to call you Renshaw. Six years ago you stole the gold of your fellow robbers in the West Indies. You settled by the merest chance in Maryport; you then posed as a rich man, rich you were certainly, and smitten with the charms of the Lady Clare, or, as I put it, knowing that she is an heiress of much wealth, you set yourself to secure her; then the money. Lord Ulric barred your way. He is a bright boy, and you resolved to kill him.

"In that you were frustrated," continued Rob Roy. "I saved Lord Ulric. Before then you arranged a false abduction. It was your men who carried the Lady Clare away, and knowing where she was—in your secret stronghold in Rannoch—you pretended to be the knight chivalrous, and rescue."

"Be careful, MacGregor," exclaimed Lord Rowelpeak. "Be careful of your statements."

"I am putting them mildly," retorted Rob Roy. "Lord Rowelpeak, if you had not such a kind heart you would be able to see further. You have been duped. Now, I will call as evidence Peter of the One Eye."

But Renshaw did not wait. Pale as death he cast a hurried glance around, and rushed from the building before Rob Roy could intercept him.

"We shall meet again," shouted Rob Roy after him. "When I descend with my clan on your stronghold you shall not know the saving quality of mercy.

CHAPTER X.

IN PURSUIT.

It was with the greatest difficulty that Rob Roy persuaded Lord Rowelpeak that Renshaw lived on the proceeds of armed bands that he retained.

"On the island of Tiree," said Rob Roy, "there is a company of wreckers who, more or less, are under his control, but his great hiding-place is in the Rannoch district. By his express orders the Lady Clare was carried away, and by the merest chance I saw her."

"You!"

"Yes, me. At the time I did not know who she was. I and my brother were hunting in the vicinity of Loch Luib, when suddenly we heard cries of distress. We followed in the trail, and it has led to here. To be particular, when I followed in the trail, I was taken prisoner, and carried to the island of Tiree.

"For some time past there have been depredations in our vicinity, and, as usual, my clan was blamed, but knowing what I know now, the blame lies at the door of the Wolf of Rannoch, Twaite, Renshaw, or whatever you care to call him.

"I can scarcely credit it," replied Lord Rowelpeak. "It looks so impossible. Renshaw has behaved himself admirably, and is well liked in the district."

"That may be," replied Rob Roy.

"But that does not alter the fact that he has been living on ill-gotten gains. He may not have taken an active interest, but his was the head that planned everything, Peter of the One-Eye acting for him at Tiree, and one Harpour, whom I fancy I have met at Rannoch. But of Rannoch I cannot speak. It is a wild, desolate region, and evidently Twaite has set up an establishment somewhere in the hills."

"When you speak of it," replied Lord Rowelpeak, "there have been innumerable robberies all over the country of late."

"And the booty has been carried to Rannoch," interjected Rob Roy. "The land north of Rannoch has been completely laid waste, and now I know the Wolf of Rannoch I shall hunt him to his lair."

"What I think of Renshaw is this," continued Rob Roy. "He is enamoured of the Lady Clare, and being a desperate man, he will move heaven and earth to carry out his designs. I should advise you, in the meantime, not to allow the Lady Clare or Lord Hazelheath out of your sight until I have reported to you that the Wolf has been captured. I must use all speed, otherwise he will escape us."

Rob Roy rose to go.

"Noble MacGregor, I would that I could ask you to accept my hospitality, but my heart tells me that instant action is necessary. I thank you from the bottom of my heart. What can I do for you at present? Shall I summon a band of my retainers to accompany you, or what do you propose?"

"I must go alone," replied Rob Roy. "No time is to be lost, and if I may borrow a pony from you I can travel quickly."

"A pony!" exclaimed Lord Rowelpeak, "you shall have the fleetest charger I have, together with a swift ed horse."

"So be it," replied Rob Roy, "I must go at once, and when you hear from me next it will be news of the discomfiture of the Wolf."

Lord Rowelpeak gave the necessary orders, and in half an hour's time Rob Roy rode from the castle on a swift horse, and a saddled led horse by his side.

CHAPTER XI.

THE ATTACK.

In four days' time Rob Roy arrived at Balquhidder, and at once sent forth the fiery cross.

In answer to that dread summons of war, the MacGregors, from the oldest greybeard to the young stripling, capable of bearing arms, seized their claymores and targes and rallied to the meeting-place.

"MacGregors," said Rob Roy, to the assembled clansmen, "we have a serious undertaking in front of us. Lately you have heard rumours of the Wolf of Rannoch, who has laid waste the country in the north. I have unearthed him, and he has two strongholds, one in Rannoch, which we have yet to discover, and the other in the island of Tiree.

"I am to divide you into three companies. All the men over sixty are to remain at home to defend our lands in case of attack; all the men between forty and sixty are to prepare at once for an expedition to the island of Tiree under Alastair; while I take you others, from eighteen to forty, to attack the Wolf's stronghold in Rannoch.

"You will find in Tiree that the stronghold is a cave, the entrance to which is a narrow and dangerous mountain pathway. But the enemy must be captured at all costs. However, I leave Alastair to deal with the matter, and when we have settled the affair at Rannoch we shall come to your assistance at Tiree. Alastair, take your party. Provision yourselves well, and good luck be with you.

"Come, men!" exclaimed Rob Roy, addressing the party of younger ones of the clan. "We must advance at once. Forward!"

With springing steps the MacGregors swung over the heather, and as evening fell Rob Roy threw out sentries, while the main body bivouacked close by.

The night passed in quietness, and in the early morning Rob Roy sent a line of skirmishers in advance, with picked scouts in front of them.

The scouts felt their way forward cautiously, when suddenly, as they came near the gully in which Rob Roy had been captured, there was a loud discharge of firearms.

The scouts and skirmishers flung themselves flat on the heather, and as Rob Roy rushed forward at the head of the main body he saw the smoke from the discharged guns slowly rising from the adjacent ridges.

"They are in strong force," muttered Rob Roy, "but we must dislodge them."

Springing to the front and waving his claymore, Rob Roy shouted the Mac-Gregor battle-cry.

"Ard Choile! Ard Choile! Follow and spare not! Follow and spare not! Forward, men! Charge!"

Like a rushing torrent the MacGregors surged forward, but the bandits did not wait. That fierce red line bearing down upon them cowed them, and after firing a few wild shots they turned and fled.

"That is Harpour, that is the leader of the masked patrol," exclaimed Rob Roy as he gained the top of the ridge and pointed towards the fleeing robbers. "But where are they going?"

Instead of making for the glen directly in front of them, the robbers swarmed up the hill on the right and disappeared over its crest.

The MacGregors were fast on their track, and hardly had the last robber disappeared over the hill than Rob Roy was standing on the ridge.

"So that is their stronghold!" exclaimed Rob Roy as the last of the robbers disappeared among the trees of a heavily-wooded plateau. "It is cunningly chosen. I can see the tops of some of the houses between the trees."

The place was cunningly chosen. Far away from the valley, which formed a natural footpath through the hills, was a plateau on a hill of moderate height. It commanded the surrounding country, but at the same time was so covered with wood and so inaccessible on account of the steepness of the surrounding hills that it formed an ideal place for concealment. The slopes of the mountain on which the stronghold stood could be easily defended from the thick undergrowth at the top, and it would take a very daring enemy to attempt to capture the position by force.

From his place of vantage Rob Roy took in all the details. "It is admirably chosen, but I must find out what the strength of the garrison is."

Ordering his clansmen to lie down out of sight, he directed the line of skirmishers to make a pretence at attack, but the moment they arrived at the foot of the hill they were met by a rapid volley from the bushes at the top.

Thanks to Rob Roy's directions, none of them was hit, for when they saw a movement in the bushes, they threw themselves flat on the ground, the bullets passing harmlessly over their heads.

"Wolf of Rannoch, Twaite, Renshaw —whatever they call you," shouted Rob Roy, "your day has come at last."

A mocking laugh rang out from the bushes. "Fool," replied the voice, "dare to approach, and your last day will have come."

Rob Roy recognised the voice. "Harpour, I know your name now," retorted Rob Roy. "Tell your master I have come to take him prisoner."

Again the mocking voice rang out: "Go home, Rob Roy, go home. You fool, the Wolf of Rannoch is not here. You may find him in Tiree or you may not. But if you attempt to force this position your blood be on your own head. We shall mow you down."

Rob Roy did not reply at once. Perhaps the man was speaking the truth. Perhaps the Wolf did go to Tiree, or, perhaps, worse luck, he might even then be hovering near Rowelpeak Castle, ready to carry off the Lady Clare at the first opportunity.

"Tell your master, for he is there," shouted Rob Roy, hazarding a guess, "that if he does not surrender I shall starve him out. I am not likely to risk the lives of my clansmen in an attempt to carry your strong position, but I shall surround you and starve you out."

In a few rapid words Rob Roy ordered his men to keep well out of sight, and to encircle the hill.

His mind was made up. To attempt to capture the position in daylight would have been madness, so he determined on a night attack.

Waiting quietly until darkness fell, Rob Roy sent round word to prepare for a simultaneous attack from all sides.

"Pass the word," whispered Rob Roy. "Advance!"

The word was quietly passed, and the MacGregors, like panthers, stealthily crept up the face of the hill on all sides.

Suddenly a stream of fire blazed from the bushes.

Rob Roy immediately sprang to the front. "Charge, men, charge!" he shouted, as the MacGregors with a loud shout crashed through the bushes.

"Strike in front, strike in front!"

shouted Rob Roy as he cut down a robber. "Strike in front, and rally round the buildings in the centre."

When the robbers discovered that the MacGregors had gained the edge of the wood, those who were able to escape from the claymores of the MacGregors rushed incontinently to the houses.

Not knowing the plan of these houses, and fearing that he might be led into a trap, Rob Roy gave the order to halt and lie down.

"Pass the word along," he whispered, "the attack will be commenced at dawn. Take good cover among the bushes."

Not a sound was to be heard save the heavy breathing of the MacGregors, and often during that night it seemed as if they were waiting by a city of the dead. The hours dragged slowly, but at last the grey morning light began to dapple over the hilltops.

Rob Roy sprang to his feet and whistled shrilly. "Forward, MacGregors! Forward! Follow and spare not!" he shouted, drawing his claymore.

In the dim light they could see several houses in a group, laid out in the form of a cross, and protected by the trees in the vicinity. From their formation they presented an admirable means of defence, and Rob Roy saw that.

But when within twenty yards of the houses, the MacGregors were brought to an abrupt standstill. All around, skilfully concealed by the undergrowth, was a strong pallisade of pointed staves, firmly fastened together. It formed a formidable barrier.

"Lie down!" thundered Rob Roy, when he saw the fearful risk his men ran of being shot down where they stood, but, strangely enough, no shot was fired from the houses.

At that moment Jorgensen ran forward. "They have fled," he exclaimed. "At least they may. I have just remembered overhearing a remark about a secret passage."

"We shall soon see," replied Rob Roy. "Bear a hand," he exclaimed as he seized the pallisading in his strong grasp. "Bear a hand. Now, altogether, heave!"

The MacGregors gave a powerful heave altogether, and the pallisade rocked in its foundations.

"Once more, men, heave!"

With a mighty pull the MacGregors tore the staves from the earth, and with a shout they rushed over the obstacle.

The houses were four in number, and not a sign of life did they show.

Rob Roy flung himself against the nearest door, but it resisted his efforts, powerful man though he was.

"Quick!" shouted Rob Roy. "Quick! Fetch one of the stanchions from the pallisade."

The stanchion was quickly brought. "Now smash in the door."

Half-a-dozen MacGregors seized the improvised battering ram, and instantly the door was knocked in splinters.

Rob Roy rushed into the room. It was plainly furnished. In the centre was a plain deal table, and Rob Roy's attention was at once arrested by a letter lying on it.

It was addressed to himself. "To Rob Roy," it said. "It is useless for you to track me down. You have spoiled my game in the meantime, but I shall be revenged. Beware! I have many secret dwelling-places, and while you were advancing to the attack, I left this place during the night by the secret entrance. I never intended staying. I wished merely to give orders to my men to meet me at a certain rendezvous. It is useless for you to go to Tiree, for I have given orders for the withdrawal of my men there. Where I go matters not, but remember, on you I shall have my revenge.—TWAITE."

"The villain signs his real name at last," said Rob Roy, "but the letter may be but a ruse. We must examine the buildings, and then follow in his track."

The other three houses had at one time been filled with valuables hastily removed, judging from the amount of precious nick-nacks lying about in confusion. But everything of great value was gone.

In the artful concealment of the place, and in the method of its construction, the Wolf of Rannoch had expended a large amount of genius.

"No doubt he will return in time," said Rob Roy, "and the proceeds of his robberies must be hidden somewhere in the vicinity. Spread yourselves out, men, and scour the country."

In the fourth room was a trap-door. Rob Roy pulled it open at once, and a moist, earthy blast fanned his cheeks.

"This is the secret passage. No doubt it leads to the foot of the hill."

As he spoke a loud "Hallo" from outside gave evidence that a discovery had been made. More than halfway down the hill was the entrance to the underground passage, which had been missed during the ascent in the darkness.

In a moment several of the more daring spirits entered it, and feeling their way, appeared below the floor at the trap-door.

"It is but a narrow passage, mostly natural," said the leading MacGregor.

"It is as I thought," replied Rob Roy. "Many of these hills are volcanic in origin and are hollow. Ha! I have an idea. Perhaps the Wolf has another hiding-place."

Another shout from outside heralded a fresh discovery. In close proximity was a conical hill covered with thick broom bushes, and on close examination it was found to be pierced by several natural tunnels.

The MacGregors poured in, and by the flash of their flintlocks in the pan they could see that in the centre was a large space piled with articles.

"A torch! a torch!" was the cry.

Rob Roy heard the shout and the cry. In a cupboard were several candles made of fir, and seizing them he rushed from the building.

When he reached the hollow mountain and lit the candles he stared in amazement.

Piles. of swords, shields, pieces of armour, guns of all description, silver plate, precious ornaments from the East, and boxes, with open ends, filled with coins met the gaze of the astonished MacGregor.

After the first surprise, Rob Roy laughed lightly.

"Well, my clansmen," he said, "it is an ill wind that blows no one any good. You will be able to decorate your houses, and we have enough money to prevent any man in the clan being in want, with a good surplus over for the poor of the neighbouring parishes."

"I must follow in the trail of the Wolf. In the meantime demolish these houses, the secret way, and carry all the spoil back to Balquihidder."

Choosing half-a-dozen of his most daring men, Rob Roy set off in pursuit of the Wolf of Rannoch.

But the Wolf was a cunning man, as Rob Roy discovered. Not far from the buildings, concealed in a wood, was a stable that had held a number of horses. These horses had recently been there,

and Rob Roy observed that they left no trace behind them.

"The cunning fox," said Rob Roy, 'has muffled the horses' feet, so as not to leave a trace behind."

They searched high and low, but it was impossile to say whether the Wolf had fled north, east, west, or south.

In this quandary Rob Roy determined at once to make for Ballachulish and thence for Tiree. Calling his men together, he set off without more ado, and by the following evening they embarked on board a fishing-boat.

When they arrived at Tiree, they were met by Alastair and his men.

"There is not a sign of life in the island," exclaimed Alastair. "By all appearance they must have left the day before we landed. They have sunk two old boats in the harbour, but that is all they have left behind."

"And the cave?" asked Rob Roy.

"We cannot find it," replied Alastair, "but we have not yet made a thorough search."

"I am not surprised you cannot find it," replied Rob Roy. "But follow me."

Rob Roy led them towards the mountain path, and giving them a word of warning he pushed forward.

It was a rash thing to do, and Rob Roy thought so when he had completed half the journey.

"What if they were to fire along the pathway from the cavern? They could massacre every one of us," he muttered, as he grasped his claymore the firmer and pressed forward rapidly.

The pathway presented no difficulty to the MacGregors, who, nimble as mountain cats, followed each other rapidly in single file.

"They have gone," exclaimed Rob Roy. "See," he shouted as he ran into the cavern. "They have left their pots and pans behind them."

It was as he said. The robbers had vanished.

"It is most disappointing," said Rob Roy; "but, at least, we have cleared the country."

"But where have they gone?" asked Alastair.

"You must ask me another," retorted Rob Roy, laughingly. "I have no idea, unless Twaite has taken into his head to repair once more to the West Indies, and become pirate again."

"The one thing we must do," continued Rob Roy, "is to destroy this place of refuge in case they ever thought of coming back."

"But you can't destroy the cavern," said Alastair.

"No," replied Rob Roy; "but I have another plan. Let us return."

When the men had reached the valley, Rob Roy asked that each man should empty half the contents of his powder flask on a large piece of canvas that he spread out.

The men did so, and making a large bundle Rob Roy climbed once more to the bridle path.

"Keep clear down below," he shouted as he placed the explosive in a niche below the level of the pathway.

Tearing out a piece of tarred rope, he lit it, and laid the unlit end on the package of powder.

Instantly he turned and ran for dear life along the pathway, but before he had reached the valley there was a blinding flash, followed by a dull roar.

In an instant the narrow footpath was demolished, and hurled into the air, together with a large part of the face of the cliff.

"That closes their retreat for ever," exclaimed Rob Roy, "for no human person can ever bridge that gulf again."

"There is nothing for it now but to return home, I suppose," said Alastair.

"That is so," replied Rob Roy, "for I must confess I am nonplussed by the movements of the Wolf. When we get home, we must make a thorough search. I shall see the MacPherson, warn the Donalds, and see all the other neighbouring chiefs. If he has gone that way he is bound to have been seen."

Rob Roy did as he said, but not a trace was seen anywhere of the Wolf of Rannoch. He disappeared as mysteriously as he came.

Dissatisfied with the search, Rob Roy journeyed to Rowelpeak Castle, but Lord Rowelpeak could offer no suggestion.

"However, as a matter of precaution I shall send the Lady Clare to London, where she will be safe in the Court of the King."

"Depend upon it," said Rob Roy, "we have not heard the last of the Wolf of Rannoch, but up to the present he has baffled me. One thing is certain, he is not in Scotland, and another thing is certain he is not in Cumberland, but wherever he may be his power is broken and his wicked designs have been thwarted."

"Thanks to you, my noble Mac-Gregor," exclaimed Lord Rowelpeak, warmly, as he wrung Rob Roy's hand. "Thanks to you. I shall keep a sharp look-out, and if I hear any tidings I shall let you know at once."

"Do so," replied Rob Roy, "and you may rely on it that the Wolf will not escape a second time."

CHAPTER XII.
BAD NEWS.

Rob Roy received news from Lord Rowelpeak sooner than he expected, for he had not been home a couple of days when a messenger arrived in hot haste with the intelligence that the Lady Clare had once more been kidnapped.

"When did this happen?" asked Rob Roy of the messenger.

"Only yesterday morning; but this letter will explain," replied the messenger, handing Rob Roy a missive from Lord Rowelpeak.

Rob Roy broke the seal and read:

DEAR MACGREGOR,—As we arranged, I sent the Lady Clare to London by postchaise. While passing through Yorkshire the chaise was attacked by highwaymen, the Lady Clare abducted, and the chaise smashed to pieces. Such is the brief news we have heard. Hasten with all speed, noble MacGregor, and earn the lasting gratitude of an anxious father.—ROWELPEAK.

"Tell Lord Rowelpeak," said Rob Roy to the messenger, "that I shall make all haste. First have a good meal, and set off with all speed. I shall follow shortly."

Rob Roy ran to his brother Alastair, and told him the news.

"It is Renshaw right enough," he said. "The wild moors of Yorkshire offer the very facilities he desires for his nefarious plans. I expect that to keep clear of the London road Lord Rowelpeak gave orders for the post-chaise to make a detour. He ought to have furnished it with a proper guard, but we shall see what we can do when we arrive at Rowelpeak Castle."

"What are you going to do?" asked Alastair.

"You and I," replied Rob Roy, "must disguise ourselves as border cattlemen. If we take any of the men suspicion would be aroused, and in any case we cannot lead an armed band into England. You and I, therefore, must start at once."

"Very good," said Alastair. "I shall run home, and don trousers and other various disguises."

In a very short time Rob Roy and Alastair had dressed themselves as cattle drovers. With thick skin caps on their heads, and to all appearance armed with nothing but a long stick, the brothers looked veritable cattlemen. But below the folds of their clothes were concealed formidable pistols, and a couple of dirks.

"It will be hand-to-hand work, Alastair, when we close," said Rob Roy. "If we manage to find a couple of swords when we cross the border, so much the better, but to take them with us now would only excite suspicion."

The journey to Rowelpeak Castle was accomplished in safety.

"Welcome, noble MacGregor," cried Lord Rowelpeak, advancing with outstretched arms. "Welcome once more, although the occasion be sad. And you, noble Alastair," continued the Earl, "I thank you for your quick response."

"We have done no more," said Alastair, "than you would have done for us."

"Now for details," said Rob Roy. "We must not lose time. Tell us the story, Lord Rowelpeak."

"Not wishing to create suspicion," said Lord Rowelpeak, "and at the request of the Lady Clare, we dispensed with a strong guard to the coach. Only two of my men accompanied it. In order to compensate for the weakness of the guard, I gave orders that the usual coach route should not be taken, but that the journey should be made through Yorkshire. Evidently they had been watched, and no sooner had they gone on the moors than they were attacked. The two guards were shot down, the coachman left for dead, the coach itself smashed up, and the Lady Clare abducted."

"Pardon me, from whom did you receive the information."

"From the coachman. He is an old servant. He was shot in the arm. The robbers thought he was killed. He fell off the box and lay quiet. In their hurry the robbers overlooked the horses. They spent too much time in breaking up the coach. They intended leaving no trace behind, and did exactly what they had not intended to do."

"Obviously," said Rob Roy, "to leave the horses was a grave error from their point of view."

"And perhaps our salvation," replied Lord Rowelpeak. "But, to continue. When Silas, the coachman, saw them depart, he caught one of the horses, and returned here with the bad news at full speed."

"Can he give any information about the men ?"

"Nothing, except that the men were all masked, well mounted, and wore grey homespun clothes."

"The description of the Wolf of Rannoch's followers," exclaimed Rob Roy.

"There can be no doubt about it from the beginning," returned Alastair. "The Wolf has been in hiding in the vicinity. Had they killed the coachman there would have been no clue."

"We must start at once, Alastair," said Rob Roy, "but first let us speak to the coachman."

"Why not take him as your guide to the moor ?" said Lord Rowelpeak.

"Exactly what I was about to suggest, my lord," replied Rob Roy.

CHAPTER XIII.

RUN TO EARTH.

Without delay Rob Roy Alastair and Silas, the coachman, set out, well mounted.

Arrived at the scene of the outrage, they gazed on the havoc created by the robbers. Not two boards of the coach were left together.

While the coachman looked sorrowfully down on the ruins of the coach, Rob Roy and Alastair were busy searching the ground in the vicinity for the trail.

"I have it!" exclaimed Rob Roy, as he completed a circle round the ruins of the coach. "I have it, and the trail leads north-east. Here," he continued, addressing the coachman. "Wait here, Silas. If we do not return by to-morrow night, make all speed to Rowelpeak Castle, and ask that reinforcements be sent without delay. Do you understand ?"

"Perfectly," replied Silas, "and I could wait here till Dooms-day if I thought that by doing so I could bring the Lady Clare back to her father."

" We shall do so," replied Rob Roy. " Come along, Alastair."

The two brothers followed the trail like sleuth-hounds, and before darkness set in they descried a solitary house far away in the distance in the wild moor.

" Be careful, Alastair," exclaimed Rob Roy. " I have no doubt that is where the Lady Clare is imprisoned, and her captors will be on the watch. Perhaps we had better rest until darkness sets in."

" A good idea," said Alastair, as he flung himself on the heather.

" Look ! " exclaimed Rob Roy, after a pause. " The house is inhabited."

As he spoke a light twinkled from one of its windows.

Waiting until darkness covered their movements, Rob Roy and Alastair crept forward with stealthy steps.

Arriving some twenty yards from the house they lay flat on the ground and waited, but no one appeared outside.

Crawling nearer, they gripped their dirks with their teeth in order to leave both hands free in an emergency.

At last they gained the walls of the house, beneath the window from which the light proceeded.

Someone inside was talking loudly. Rob Roy cautiously drew his head level with the window, but the thick curtain prevented him seeing anyone.

" I hate you ; I despise you ; I dare you to do your worst ! " said the voice of a woman.

" Hist, Alastair," whispered Rob Roy. " It is the Lady Clare."

A mocking laugh was the answer to the young girl's words.

" My pretty beauty," said a voice that Rob Roy at once recognised as that of Renshaw, " my pretty beauty, before I have done with you I will tame your spirit. To-morrow we leave this house, and in the morning we sail for the West Indies, where you shall adorn the home as a pirate's bride."

" I scorn you," replied the Lady Clare.

" Tempt me not," said Renshaw, with a savage ring in his voice. " Tempt me not further, for woman as you are and madly as I love you, you will force me to deal roughly with you."

" Love me ! " exclaimed the girl with bitter sarcasm. " Love ! Why, you wretch, you know not of what you talk."

" Burst the door, Alastair," whispered Rob Roy. Alastair and Rob Roy crept to the door and flung themselves upon it. In an instant it was burst open, and the two Highlanders rushed into the presence of the scowling Renshaw and the Lady Clare.

Renshaw was completely taken by surprise.

" Rob Roy ! " he gasped.

" Yes. We meet at last," returned Rob Roy, advancing threateningly towards Renshaw.

" Alastair," continued Rob Roy, quickly, " take the Lady Clare from the room while I deal with this scoundrel."

" You shall not ! " yelled Renshaw, springing forward, with hatred depicted on every feature of his face. " You shall not ! Take that."

As he sprang forward, he levelled a pistol and fired. But Rob Roy was too quick for him. Like lightning he drew his pistol and fired. Two shots rang out, and as the smoke cleared away Rob Roy was standing unharmed with Renshaw, the Wolf of Rannoch, lying dead at his feet with a bullet through his brain.

" He brought about his own ruin," muttered Rob Roy. " Come, Alastair, let us hie to Rowelpeak Castle without delay."

By morning they regained Silas, the coachman, and together they journeyed to the Castle where the safe arrival of the Lady Clare occasioned unbounded joy.

THE END.

Published by JAMES HENDERSON & SONS, at Red Lion House, Red Lion-court, Fleet-street, E.C.

www.ingramcontent.com/pod-product-compliance
Lightning Source LLC
Chambersburg PA
CBHW082054220626

47052CB00006B/1234